Westwood Elementary School
883 Cross St.
Portland, Mich. 48875

{Katharine the Almost Great}

Can't Keep Trackula of Jackula

by Lisa Mullarkey
illustrated by Phyllis Harris

magic
wagon

visit us at www.abdopublishing.com

To my nephew, Jack Petitt: the real Jackula!—LM

To Janet DeCarlo. Thank you! —PH

Published by Magic Wagon, a division of the ABDO Group, 8000 West 78th Street, Edina, Minnesota 55439. Copyright © 2009 by Abdo Consulting Group, Inc. International copyrights reserved in all countries. All rights reserved. No part of this book may be reproduced in any form without written permission from the publisher.

Calico Chapter Books™ is a trademark and logo of Magic Wagon.

Printed in the United States.

Text by Lisa Mullarkey
Illustrations by Phyllis Harris
Edited by Stephanie Hedlund and Rochelle Baltzer
Interior layout and design by Jaime Martens
Cover design by Jaime Martens

Library of Congress Cataloging-in-Publication Data

Mullarkey, Lisa.
  Can't keep trackula of Jackula / by Lisa Mullarkey ; illustrated by Phyllis Harris.
    p. cm. -- (Katharine the almost great ; bk. 6)
  ISBN 978-1-60270-584-5
  [1. Halloween--Fiction. 2. Schools--Fiction.] I. Harris, Phyllis, 1962- ill. II. Title.
  PZ7.M91148Can 2009
  [E]--dc22
                                                  2008036090

❋ CONTENTS ❋

❋ CHAPTER 1 ❋

Spook-a-Rama Drama

Halloween is the most super-duper holiday of the year. Except for Christmas. And my birthday. And Valentine's Day. Those itty-bitty hearts with sayings like URAQT are gr8!

Still, Halloween is spooktacular. But I have a teensy-weensy secret. Monsters and ghosts give me spook-a-rama trick-or-treat drama. I do not like them. Not one bit. Not that I believe in those things . . . anymore.

So when I saw the Dracula DVD that Crockett brought upstairs for movie night, my hands started to sweat.

"That looks scary," I said nervously.

Since Crockett is usually nice about things that creep me out, I thought he'd say this:

"Okay, we can watch a Penelope Parks movie."

But he didn't. Instead, he said:

"Dracula isn't real, you know. Don't be a scaredy-cat."

"I know he's not real," I said as I nibbled my nails. But the truth was, Dracula was one of the reasons I wasn't getting rid of my can of Monsters-Be-Gone spray anytime soon. I took a deep breath and scrunched my nose. "Go ahead. Put it in."

I looked at the cover again. "Did you know that one of the smallest mammals in the world is the bumblebee bat?"

Crockett's eyes lit up. "Actually, I knew that." He shoved the DVD into the player. "Who's the most famous ghost detective in the world?"

I tossed a piece of popcorn into my mouth and shrugged.

"Sherlock Moans!" Crockett said and then laughed. "Get it?"

"Got it," I said.

Crockett tapped the dog next to Dracula on the DVD case. "What kind of dog does Dracula want?" He folded his arms and tapped his foot. "A bloodhound."

Halloween was only a week away. That meant apple pie, carved pumpkins, and for some reason, Crockett's endless Halloween jokes.

Mom climbed over the kitchen gate and plopped Jack on the floor.

"Jack's as cranky as a witch without her broom. Maybe he'll sit with you kids for a while."

"It's movie night," I whined. "Besides, Jack doesn't sit anymore." It was true. Jack crawled, cruised, and crept around the house. He was an expert at knocking over plants, bumping his head, and pushing everything off of the coffee table.

His new trick was getting stuck under the coffee table. He'd roll under but couldn't roll out. He'd cry until someone rescued him. But once he was free, he'd scootch-a-roo right back under.

Crockett wiped the disgust-o drool off of Jack's chin. "He looks happy now."

Mom climbed back over the gate. "If he gets cranky, let me know."

But Jack didn't get cranky. His eyes were glued to the TV.

"Do you think he likes it?" I asked Crockett. "Is it too scary?"

"He's a baby," said Crockett. "He doesn't know it's supposed to be scary."

Whenever Dracula flashed his fangs, Jack clapped his hands.

When Dracula chased the mummy, Jack bounced and gurgled. When Dracula said, "I w a n t to suck y o u r blood," Jack said, "Yeth."

"Let's watch it again!" said Crockett when it ended.

"No way," I said. "Too spooky."

Jack cried. He crawled across the floor and pulled himself up on the kitchen gate. Mom scooped him up. "There's my boo-tiful baby!"

Crockett took out the DVD. "I'm going downstairs to watch it again."

After his parents got divorced, Crockett and Aunt Chrissy moved into our basement. Since Crockett had all sorts of creepy crawlers downstairs, I stayed upstairs in the critter-free zone.

Before Crockett ran downstairs, he told another joke. "Why did the vampire quit the baseball team? Because they would only let him be *bat* boy. Get it?"

It was going to be a long week.

After Crockett left, I zip-a-zoomed around the house and flicked on every light.

"Did the movie scare you?" Mom asked as she rocked Jack back and forth. I shook my head.

Mom raised her eyebrow. "Would you feel better falling asleep on the couch?" She wiped more drool from Jack's mouth. "Jack's been acting so strange, I'm sure he'll be up for a while."

A minute later, I was comfy cozy with my pillow and blanket. I fell asleep listening to Mom reminding me that monsters weren't real. I drifted off to sleep believing it until . . .

"*Ouch!*" I screamed. I shot up and rubbed my eyes. "Double ouch!" I shouted again. Someone or something had bitten my toe . . . twice!

Looking down, I saw the monster's mouth still munching away!

It was Jack! He flashed his pointy teeth. Teeth that were *not* there this morning! My stomach did a flip-flop belly drop. In that second, I knew that the baby looking back at me wasn't Jack.

It was *Jackula*!

My brother had turned into a baby vampire!

❀ CHAPTER 2 ❀

A Pain in the Neck!

"Let go of Katharine's toe," said Mom as she swooped into the room.

But Jackula chomp-a-chewed harder.

Finally, I snatched my foot away. "Jack has teeth! Sharp teeth!"

Mom rubbed my toe. "That explains why he's been so cranky."

Jackula crawled over to the TV and sucked on the corner of the DVD case. "More."

I slapped my forehead. "We're doomed. DOOMED! Jack's a vampire.

He has fangs! He's turned into . . . Jackula."

Mom scooped Jackula off of the floor. "Don't be so dramatic, Katharine. He's teething. When babies teethe, they bite."

Mom always says I'm too dramatic. That's one of the reasons my parents call me Katharine the *Almost* Great. They say I'm a work-in-progress. Maybe if I stopped being the drama queen they thought I was, they'd call me Katharine the Great once and for all.

Jackula licked his lips. "More, more, more," he said as he crawled toward me.

I swung my feet over his head and tucked them underneath my legs. "No!"

Jackula laughed. "Yeth."

Crockett flew up the stairs. "What's wrong, Katharine? You look like you've seen a ghost."

"Worse!" I said. "A vampire! He's Jackula!"

Mom shot me a look. "Katharine, I don't want to hear any nonsense about vampires." Then she added in her thundery voice, "Stop calling him Jackula."

Crockett squatted and looked Jackula right in the eye. This is what I thought he'd say:

"He does have that evil vampire look. He looks like he vants to suck our blood."

But he said this:

"Do you swear to tell the tooth, the whole tooth, and nothing but the tooth?" Then he kissed Jackula! "If you're hungry, you need to eat where little vampires eat. You know where that is?"

Jackula burped.

"The casketeria!" said Crockett.

This was not a chuckle moment.

Jack chomped at the air. I was pretty sure if he had the chance, he'd sink his fangs into me again.

"I'm outta here," I said as I skedaddled to my room and locked the door. Thanks to my can of Monsters-Be-Gone Spray from first grade, I knew I'd be safe . . . for now.

When I woke up the next day, Dad and Aunt Chrissy were looking in Jackula's mouth while Mom cooked breakfast.

"He has four teeth," said Aunt Chrissy. "They're multiplying faster than the dust bunnies under my bed."

At least the Tooth Fairy would be happy.

"Ouch!" shouted Aunt Chrissy. "He bit me." She shook her finger at Jackula. "No biting. No."

Jackula clapped his hands. "Yeth." He yawned.

Then Dad yawned. "He didn't sleep again last night. He's been up nights and sleeping during the day."

"Just like Dracula!" I shrieked. I walked over to his high chair. "Are you Jackula? A baby vampire?"

"Yeth." He drooled some more.

That's when I noticed Jackula's breakfast. Bat- and pumpkin-shaped pancakes!

I snatched the bat pancakes off of his plate. "No bat pancakes for you."

Mom gave me her grumpy, grumpy eyes. "Knock it off, Katharine."

I lifted the pumpkin pancakes and slid the bats underneath. "Don't eat the bats," I whispered.

Jackula clapped. A second later, he had a big goof-a-roo grin plastered on his face. He tossed the pumpkin pancakes on the floor and gobbled up the bats!

Just then, Crockett came upstairs with the Dracula DVD in his hand. "Hey there, Jack." He put the DVD on the counter, leaned in, and put his forehead on Jack's. Jackula grabbed Crockett's face and bit him on the nose.

"Owwww!" shouted Crockett, rubbing his nose. "He bit me. Maybe he is Jackula!"

Aunt Chrissy giggled. "That's what happens when you get too close to a baby who's teething."

I grabbed the DVD off the counter and held it up. When Jack saw it, he kicked his feet and cooed. He pointed at Dracula and said, "Da Da."

Dad lifted Jackula out of his high chair. "Hey, buddy. That's not your Da Da. I am."

"No, no, no!" Jackula cried. He wiggled so much that Dad had to put him on the floor before he dropped him.

Jackula crept under the table and made slurping sounds.

I ate my pancakes standing up so I could see him. I tried warning everyone about Jackula, but they ignored me.

Jackula peeked out from under the table and smiled. Then, like a flash of lightning, he sunk his fangs into Dad's ankle!

Dad jumped. "No, Jack. No biting." Then he looked at Mom. "Carol, look at Jack. He has an odd look in his eyes."

"They're vampire eyes," I said. "He looks like the vampire kid in the movie."

"Don't be silly," said Dad.

"Don't be so dramatic," said Mom.

"Pass the pancakes," said Crockett.

The rest of the day, I avoided Jackula. If he was in the living room, I stayed in the dining room. If he went outside, I stayed inside. But it was hard to keep trackula of Jackula!

I was too worried about another attack to eat dinner. I thought about the biting. The sucking and slurping. The bat pancakes. Not sleeping at night . . .

After dinner, I made a Beware of Jackula sign and taped it to my bedroom door.

When Dad tucked me in, he swiped the sign off the door and flapped it under my nose.

"Your brother is not a vampire," Dad said in a thundery voice. "He's teething."

I fluff-a-puffed my pillow. "Did you know that George Washington didn't really have wooden teeth? His fake teeth were made from the tusk of a hippopotamus."

Dad kissed my forehead. "Like I said, Jack's teething."

Ha! I knew the truth. Jack was gone and Jackula was a pain in the neck!

In fact, he was driving me batty!

❊ CHAPTER 3 ❊

Miss Priss-A-Poo to the Rescue

B y the time Monday came, I was hap-hap-happy to escape Jackula's jaws. I even went to school early to help Mom make lunch. That's when I heard her talking on the phone to my old second grade teacher, Ms. Cerra.

Mom yawned. "I have to face facts. He's not sleeping. I'll have to buy him one."

They were talking about Jackula! Just then, Mom turned on the blender and I couldn't hear the rest . . . except for one word: coffin! Mom was buying Jackula a coffin!

I couldn't wait to tell Crockett!

When school started, Mrs. Bingsley called us to the carpet. She held up the book *Dracula Goes to the Dentist*. I bit my lip and sighed.

"What's wrong, Katharine?"

I gulped. "Do you think vampires are real, Mrs. Bingsley?"

She put the book down. "No. This is a funny, made-up story. It's fiction."

Vanessa Garfinkle, aka Miss Priss-A-Poo, twisted her hair around her finger. "Are you scared of vampires, Katharine?"

Everyone waited for my answer. "Did you know that the average person has 100,000 hairs on their head?"

Johnny started to count the strands on Rebecca's head. Tamara smacked Matthew's hand away from her hair.

Usually, an amazing fact from my calendar of 365 useless facts rescued me. But not this time. Miss Priss-A-Poo asked again. "Are you afraid of vampires?"

I picked at a scab on my knee. "Everyone knows that only little kids believe in stuff like that. You know, like goo-goo ga-ga babies."

Miss Priss-A-Poo's shoulders slumped.

Crockett's hand shot into the air. "Why doesn't anyone like Dracula? Because he has a bat temper!"

Mrs. Bingsley smiled and shuffled through a stack of Halloween books on the floor. She pulled out *The Pumpkin Patch Mystery*. "I think this book might be a better choice."

And it was.

❀ ❀ ❀

During recess, I didn't play four square or squash the leaves. I grabbed

Crockett's hand and marched over to the picnic tables.

"This morning, my mom told Ms. Cerra that she was buying Jackula a coffin!"

Crockett's eyes grew wide. "Are you sure she said coffin?"

I nodded. "She said Jackula's not sleeping at night. Then she said coffin. She must be getting him one so he'll let her sleep!" My eyes filled with tears. "I want Jack back."

Crockett scratched his head. Before he said anything, I heard a sneeze coming from the other side of the trash can.

"Who's there?" I demanded.

Miss Priss-A-Poo stuck her head out. "It's me."

"Are you being a snooper pooper again?" I asked. "Did you hear anything?"

This is what I thought she'd say:

"Who's the baby now?   You *do* believe in vampires!"

But she didn't. She held out her sketchbook and said:

"I'm not a snooper pooper.   I'm drawing."

I gave Crockett my do-not-say-another-word-to-Miss-Priss-A-Poo eyes.

Then, the bell rang and we ran to the doors.

That afternoon, we had library time with Mr. Ray. As I looked through the Penelope Parks books, I heard a whisper.

"Katharine, over here."

Behind a tall bookshelf, I saw Vanessa peeking through a stack of books. She looked to the left and then to the right. "Meet me by the computers. Come alone."

What was Vanessa up to now?

When I got there, she shoved a thick folder marked PRIVATE into my hand.

"Don't open it here," she whispered. "Wait until you're home. Alone." Then she vanished like a ghost.

Waiting to open it would be easy breezy since I'm a fab-u-lo-so waiting-to-open-it-up type of kid."

Except on Christmas morning. I'm supposed to wait until everyone wakes up before opening my gifts. But I don't. I can't help taking a sneak peek before the sun comes up.

And I really can't stop myself from ripping open my report card envelope on the way home from school even though it's stamped FOR PARENTS' EYES ONLY.

I glanced at Mrs. Bingsley. She said anyone who wanted to be nominated for Student Council in the future had to be honest and trustworthy. Since I wanted to be fourth grade president next year, I needed to work extra hard.

I glanced at the folder from Vanessa. Here was my chance! I shoved it in my Penelope Parks book and didn't think about it again until the bell rang.

As soon as I got home, I ran to my room and locked the door. I yanked the folder out of my backpack. Inside was the book *101 Ways to Tame Monster Siblings*. There was a note on a sticky yellow piece of paper.

Katharine,

Looks can be deceiving. My brother acted like a monster, too. It's too scary to talk about. Trust me. Good luck and be careful!

Vanessa

Miss Priss-A-Poo had heard everything! She knew my secret! I clenched my fists.

A picture of Vanessa and her two-year-old brother, Frankie, fluttered out of the book. Some kids teased Vanessa and called her brother Square Head Boy.

I studied the picture and noticed that he did have a square head. His skin looked odd, too. Greenish.

When I flipped over the picture, someone had written Vanessa and Frankie Jr. in grown-up writing.

But scribbled underneath, in Vanessa's handwriting, was Vanessa and *Frankiestein*!

That's when I knew . . .

Frankie was a monster, too!

QUIZ: Is a Vampire Hanging
Around Your House?

1. Does your sibling sleep during the day and stay
awake at night? YES!

2. Does your sibling bite, suck, and slurp everything
in sight? YES!

3. Does your sibling have a fondness for bats?
YES! Bat Pancakes!

4. Can your sibling see his own reflection?
I don't know.

5. Does your sibling brush his teeth a lot? Jack
just got his teeth. He doesn't
brush yet.

❀ CHAPTER 4 ❀

Double Trouble

I immediately opened up *101 Ways to Tame Monster Siblings. Vampires* stood out on the contents page. I flipped to Chapter 4.

There was a quiz, which I took quicky quick. Then, I plucked my Penelope Parks mirror off my nightstand and shoved it in my pocket. Jackula was about to flunk his first test!

I kept reading. It said: *If you answered yes to at least three questions, you have a vampire for a brother or sister. WARNING! Take action now!*

Since I was ready for action, I read the first step:

Step 1: Eat garlic. NOW. For the next 24 hours, eat as much garlic as you can. Vampires don't like garlic and won't come within ten feet of you. Make a garlic clove necklace. Do not take it off.

Step 2: Reread Step 1. What are you waiting for? Don't turn the page to see Step 3 until Step 1 is finished. Be brave! Good luck! You're going to need it!

I shut the book and sniffed the air. Pasta sauce! I zip-a-zoomed to the kitchen. Mom was stirring the sauce in a pot. "You look tired, Mom."

She yawned. "I am. Jack hasn't been sleeping, but maybe that will change once we get a new mattress."

She couldn't fool me. Mattress must be secret code for coffin.

I pulled out a chair and jumped back. Jackula was under the table drinking a bottle. "You scared me!"

Jackula threw his bottle on the floor. Mom rushed over and grabbed it. "He almost bit through the nipple. His bottle days may be over soon."

I tried to get a closer look at the bottle. Was that red liquid inside? Jack only drank milk or water! "What's inside that bottle?" I asked.

"Just trying something new for Jack." She untwisted the lid and poured the liquid down the drain.

It was blood! Thick blood!

Aunt Chrissy brought the mail inside and sat down at the table.

"Ouch!" She looked under the table. "Jack bit me. I didn't know he was under there."

I whispered. "It's hard to keep trackula of Jackula."

Mom slammed the cabinet door and glared at me.

My voice cracked. "How about I set the table while you both take Jack outside and relax?"

Mom hesitated. "I could use a break." She scooped Jackula up and headed outside.

Once they were outside, I grabbed a jar of minced garlic out of the fridge and a bottle of garlic powder from the spice rack.

As I lifted the lid off of the sauce, a yummy smell filled the room. My stomach growled. I unscrewed the lid off the minced garlic and dumped the entire jar in the sauce. With a few quick stirs, presto change! You couldn't tell it was there.

Then I took the salad bowl out of the fridge and shook garlic powder on top. It smelled fab-u-lo-so! Whenever I thought about Jackula's sharp fangs, I shook faster. Before I knew it, the entire bottle was mixed into the salad.

The only other garlic left were the cloves in the pantry. I shoved three into my other pocket to make the necklace later.

When everyone sat at the table, Dad sniffed the air. "Sure smells . . . good."

Mom crinkled her nose. "I may have used too much garlic."

Crockett picked up his fork. "What does a skeleton order for dinner?"

"What?" asked Aunt Chrissy taking a bite.

"Spare ribs!" said Crockett plunging his fork into a tomato.

Aunt Chrissy dropped her fork. "Whoa! Carol, something's wrong."

Mom tasted her noodles. "Oh! There's way too much garlic in here."

Crockett reached for his water. "The salad's gross, too!"

I shoveled the food into my mouth. If they wanted to escape Jackula's jaws, they'd stop complaining and start eating.

"How can you eat it?" asked Crockett.

"I love it! Garlic's good for you and it will keep Jacku . . ."

Mom tossed her napkin on her plate. "Katharine, did you put extra garlic in here because you think your brother is a vampire?"

I gave her my very most innocent look. "Did you know that each person eats an average of 2.6 pounds of garlic a year?"

Dad wiped his mouth. "Is it usually all in one meal?"

Mom plucked a jar of white sauce out of the pantry. "I'll heat this up. My sauce is ruined."

I pushed my plate away and licked my lips. "I love, love, love that sauce."

Mom smiled. I thought she'd say:

"It will be ready in a minute."

But she didn't. Instead, she pushed my plate back and said:

"Oh, no you don't, Katharine. You made this mess. You eat it."

"That's a fitting punishment," said Dad. "That and playing with Jack after dinner."

Me . . . and Jackula? I clutched my neck and tried to smile.

As I got up to get my third glass of water, my Penelope Parks mirror popped out of my pocket and crashed to the floor. It shattered into a gazillion pieces.

I was doomed! Doomed! First Jackula, now this!

Jackula + seven years bad luck = Double Trouble!

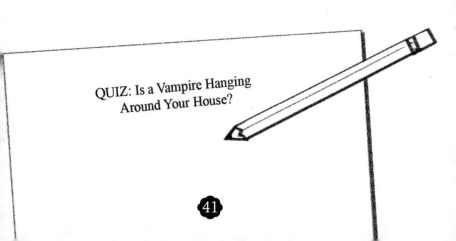

QUIZ: Is a Vampire Hanging
Around Your House?

CHAPTER 5

The Nose Knows

Garlic didn't keep Jackula away. But it kept all of my friends away the next day. I caused all sorts of stink-a-rama smelly drama!

"What smells awful?" asked Johnny as he sniffed the air.

Rebecca covered her nose. "It's gross."

"It smells like garlic," said Matthew. "I think it's coming from Katharine." He ran his hand over my necklace. "Is that garlic around your neck?"

Kids backed up as they waved away the air in front of their faces. I cleared my throat. "Did you know that a giraffe's neck is about 6 feet long and weighs 600 pounds?"

"Who cares?" said Lily as she waved her hand in front of her nose. "Why are you wearing garlic around your neck?"

I twirled my pigtails. "Because I want to!" I skipped back to my seat.

A minute later, Vanessa threw a note on my desk.

Dear Katharine,

When I had to get rid of Frankiestein, I scared him away with mint. I made dental floss necklaces and bracelets to wear. Sorry yours has to be so stinky!

Vanessa

Great. I get stuck with stink-o, disgust-o garlic while Vanessa got to smell minty fresh.

Mrs. Bingsley came in and closed the door behind her. After the Pledge of Allegiance, she wrinkled her nose. "Does anyone smell garlic?"

Everyone pointed to me. I clutched my necklace.

I thought she'd say this:

"A garlic necklace? Are you crazy? Garlic belongs in pasta sauce. Not around your neck."

But she said:

"I love the smell of garlic. I used to make garlic necklaces around Halloween, too."

Mrs. Bingsley sure did know how to make me feel fab-u-lo-so!

"Speaking of Halloween," said Mrs. Bingsley. "Today is the Student Council's first Halloween Costume Swap. Anyone participating may pick out a costume after lunch."

I crossed my fingers and hoped Rebecca's Penelope Parks costume would be there.

"I want to thank Crockett for the idea," said Mrs. Bingsley. "It was part of his Going Green platform. It's a great way to save money *and* recycle."

Everyone clapped.

Crockett bowed and squeezed in a few more jokes. "Where do ghosts go during the day?"

Elizabeth yelled out, "DaySCARE centers."

He looked at Mrs. Bingsley. "Can I tell one more joke?"

She nodded.

"What's a ghost's favorite ride at the carnival?"

Everyone shouted, "A roller *ghoster!*" Everyone but me. I had more important things to think about.

During recess, I snuck Vanessa's book outside. I squished under the slide so no one could see me and read Step 3.

Step 3: Get Proof. When you tell your family that you suspect a most unpleasant monster in the house, they won't believe you. But WE believe you! Do not dare tell your friends or discuss it further with family until you have enough evidence to prove it. If you don't have proof, how will you convince them?

Think like a detective! Collect clues! When I discovered my brother was a werewolf, I gathered his fangs and fur, taped him howling at the moon, and snapped pictures of his furry palms. It's that easy. But be forewarned: collecting evidence can be dangerous.

If you survive, read Step 4 tomorrow. No matter what happens, do not let your monster see another. Under ANY circumstances! If they do, your monster will multiply rapidly! Good luck, my friend!

When the bell rang, I tucked the book inside the PRIVATE folder and skedaddled to the door.

Two minutes later, our class headed toward the library for our costumes.

Crockett was at the front of the line. He stopped at the door and announced, "Remember, you can only take one costume unless you're getting one for baby brothers or sisters. There are tons of baby costumes."

When he opened the door, Mr. Ray was waiting in his Cat in the Hat costume. "Take your time. There's a huge selection."

The library looked spook-a-riffic! Black and orange streamers hung from the ceiling. Fake cobwebs covered the bookcases. In the corner, Ms. Cerra danced to the "Monster Mash" with her second graders.

I walked around the room and spied a whole section of Penelope Parks costumes full of glitter! I'd shine, shine, shine! But then my heart went thumpity thump when I noticed what was behind the Penelope Parks costumes. Vampire outfits. Too many to count! Humongous ones. Itty-bitty ones. Red ones. Black ones.

I thought of Step 3: "No matter what you do, do not let your monster see another. Under ANY circumstances! If they do, your monster will multiply rapidly!

My stomach did a flip-flop belly drop. Aunt Chrissy was bringing Jackula to our Halloween Parade. He couldn't see any of these costumes!

Then I got a super-duper idea. A how-to-save-the-whole-school-from-vampires idea. I opened my bag and stuffed every one of those vampire costumes inside quicky quick. Soon, the capes, fangs, fake blood, makeup, and wigs were safely hidden.

I felt a teensy-weensy bit better until I felt a tap, tap, tap on my shoulder. I swung around and saw our principal, Mrs. Ammer. She snatched my bag and pointed to the door.

Nailed by *Ammer the Hammer* . . . again.

❀ CHAPTER 6 ❀

Stealie Girl Wants Her Mummy!

Mrs. Ammer's office looked like Invasion of the Pumpkin People. Pumpkins lined her desk, table, and windowsill.

Behind her desk was a sign that said *Welcome to the Pumpkin Patch.* Next to the phone was a teeny-tiny pumpkin with a black cat standing next to it. The cat's eyes were sparkly, glittery green. A sign around the cat's neck said, I've Got My Eye on You!

Mrs. Ammer sat down and stared at me. Her eyes were the same color as the cat's!

I whispered, "Did you know that cats have 290 bones and 517 muscles in their bodies?"

Mrs. Ammer did not look impressed with my cat facts. She plopped the bag of costumes on her desk. "Katharine, can you explain this?"

"I can't," I said.

"What do you mean you *can't*?" said Mrs. Ammer. "Can't or won't?"

I thought long and hard about the difference between can't and won't. Finally, I repeated, "I can't."

"You knew the rules," Mrs. Ammer said calmly. "One costume per person. Did you understand that rule?"

I nodded.

"And you deliberately ignored the rule and put . . . ," She paused to count them. "*Nine* vampire costumes in your bag?"

I nodded again.

"That's stealing, Katharine."

Stealing? I wasn't a Stealie Girl! Except for the time when I didn't pass go but still collected $200. And the time I accidentally saw the answer to a math problem on Crockett's test and borrowed it.

"I wasn't stealing, Mrs. Ammer. Honest. I'm a fair and square kind of kid . . . now."

She raised her eyebrows.

"Really!" I said twisting my pigtails. "If I'm going to get nominated for Student Council next year, I need to be honest. I know I can't do that if I steal."

"Well, if it's not stealing," said Mrs. Ammer, "what is it?"

I slouched over. "You won't believe me. The book said . . ." Then I covered my mouth. "Oops!"

"What book?" asked Mrs. Ammer. She scribbled notes on a piece of candy corn shaped paper.

"I can't tell you," I said swinging my feet back and forth. "It's sort of a secret."

She scribbled faster. "So, you're not going to tell me why you took all of these costumes?"

I thought of the book and Jackula. I had to get Jack back! I shuffled my feet. "Sorry."

Mrs. Ammer frowned. "If that's how you feel about it." She stood and motioned for me to stand too.

I thought she would say this:

"You're a fair and square kind of kid. Let's forget about it."

But she didn't. She said:

"Your parade privileges are suspended. You can't participate in the

Halloween party or march in the parade."

My eyes burned.

"If you change your mind and share your reasons as to why you took nine costumes, I'll reconsider."

I needed proof and planned on getting it! I just hoped I could do it in time to be in the parade.

"Can I tell you on Friday morning?" I asked. "I need to do something first."

Mrs. Ammer nodded.

Part of me hoped Mom would burst-a-rooni through the door and explain everything to Mrs. Ammer. But if she knew Mrs. Ammer thought I was a Stealie Girl, I'd be in mucho mega trouble.

I crossed my fingers. "Do you have to tell my mom?"

Mrs. Ammer rubbed her chin and sighed. "I'm hoping I can trust you, Katharine." She threw her hands up into the air. "I'll give you until Friday morning to convince me you had a good reason to take those costumes."

I hug-a-rooed Mrs. Ammer. "You won't be sorry, Mrs. Ammer. I might have just saved the whole school from turning into . . . ," I zipped my lips and shoved my hands in my pockets. "I'll see you Friday morning."

Before I left, she winked and pointed to the sign around the cat's neck. *I've Got My Eye on You!*

I thought of Jackula. Having eyes on me was much better than teeth!

When I got back to my classroom, everyone was trying on their costumes. Rebecca and Tamara were matching M&Ms. Matthew and Johnny were ninjas. Caroline and Elizabeth were eggs and bacon. Crockett was wearing a George Washington costume.

"Get it, Katharine?" said Crockett. "I'm a president!" Then his eyes lit up. "What did George Washington dress up as on Halloween?"

I wasn't in the mood for another joke. I turned away and almost bumped into Abe Lincoln. "I'm the sixteenth president," said Sam as I sat down in my seat.

I tried to smile but I couldn't.

Zach, Diego, and Julia were pirates. Julia had picked out my pirate queen outfit from last year.

Haley and Addison slipped on their penguin costumes and waddled around the classroom.

Vanessa tiptoed over. "I saw what happened," she said. "Did you get in trouble for being a Stealie Girl?"

"I don't want to talk about it," I said, dropping my head on my desk.

"But I understand," said Vanessa. "I would have done the same exact thing."

I peeked out from under my arm. "Really?"

Vanessa nodded. "You saved a lot of people from turning into vampires today. Mrs. Ammer should be thanking you. So should Diego and Matthew. They were looking for Dracula costumes. If they only knew . . ."

"How's Frankie?" I asked. "Is he still . . . Frankiestein?"

Vanessa hissed. "I told you I don't want to talk about it."

She stood and looked like she was about to cry. "Just follow the directions in the book. Good luck."

I thought of the shattered mirror. It would be seven years before I had good luck again.

Seven.

Long.

Years.

CHAPTER 7

The Proof Goes Poof

On the way home, I told Crockett about my visit with Mrs. Ammer.

Crockett stopped walking. "Maybe I can help. I shouldn't bring this up but . . ."

Crockett looked over his shoulder. "I was recycling newspapers last night while your mom was outside on her cell phone. The window was open. She said something about Transylvania and the Vampire Stake Building."

I gulped. "Transylvania is where Dracula lives!" I took a deep breath and counted to five. "He must live in the Vampire Stake Building." I sighed. Collecting evidence should be easy breezy.

And it was. I slinked, skulked, and slithered around the house. I peered, prodded, and poked around every corner.

After dinner, I announced, "I have proof Jackula's a vampire. Follow me."

Mom groaned. Dad grumbled. Aunt Chrissy smirked.

Everyone trudged upstairs. I flung my door open and grabbed the bottle on the bed. "Exhibit A: blood juice."

"It's *tomato juice*," said Mom.

I stuck out my tongue and crinkled my nose. "Tomato juice is gag-a-rooni."

"I didn't want you bad-mouthing it in front of Jack," said Mom. "So, I didn't mention it." She snatched the bottle from my hand. "It's *not* blood."

"It looks like blood," said Crockett.

"Looks can be deceiving," said Aunt Chrissy.

I held the bat cookie cutter up in the air. "Why did Jackula only eat the bat-shaped pancakes?"

Mom laughed. "It could have had something to do with the sugar and cinnamon I added to the batch of bats."

"What about this?" I asked, waving a new toothbrush in the air.

Dad grabbed it. "Since Jack has teeth, we have to brush them, don't we?"

I whipped out a notebook. "Last night, Crockett heard Mom mention the Vampire Stake Building in Transylvania."

Aunt Chrissy rolled her eyes. "Pop Pop's vacationing in *Pennsylvania* next month. Next time he visits, we're taking him to the Empire State Building."

Oops!

"What about Jackula's coffin, Mom? You told Ms. Cerra that you were buying him one."

Mom's eyes grew wide. "Katharine, you do have an active imagination! Jack was cough*ing*. I'm buying him a new mattress. The one we have isn't firm enough. Maybe he'll sleep better."

This wasn't going like I had planned. "So mattress isn't a code word for coffin?"

"No," said Mom and Dad together.

Double oops!

"Tell her, Carol," said Dad. "She deserves to hear the truth . . . once and for all."

"The tooth, the whole tooth, and nothing but the tooth?" asked Crockett.

Were they going to spill the beans? Finally fess up? Admit we have a baby vampire who's driving me batty?

"Hmm," said Mom. "Maybe we shouldn't."

I stomped my foot on the ground. "You should! I'm having freak-a-rama vampire drama."

Aunt Chrissy spoke up. "Let's show her."

So they did. We went downstairs and Dad popped in a DVD.

A second later, squished doughnuts were plastered across the screen. They were scattered on the kitchen floor. A box marked Jelly Doughnuts lay near them.

"Why am I looking at jelly doughnuts?" I asked.

"Just wait," said Dad fast-forwarding the DVD. "Here it comes."

The camera zoomed in to show a close-up of Jack with red gunk around his mouth. "Disgust-o!" Jackula looked like an ooey, gooey, gunky mess!

Aunt Chrissy laughed. "Look at that little monster! All the jelly was slurped out of a dozen doughnuts!"

My stomach did a flip-flop belly drop. Was more proof that Jack was Jackula supposed to make me feel better?

Dad fast-forwarded some more until it showed Mom and Jack in a rocking chair. Mom pointed a clock toward the camera, "It's 3 AM and our little one, at four months old, is *still* refusing to go to bed."

So he *never* slept at night? This was worse than I thought! He'd been getting ready to turn into Jackula for months and I didn't even know it!

But the last scene was the scariest of all. Dad was showing off bite marks on his shoulder. Then he said, "Let me tape your bite mark. Chrissy and Carol won't believe the size of it."

Then the camera got wobbly. Finally, Dad zoomed in on someone's bite mark. The camera slowly pulled away. It was Crockett's father! He'd never even seen Jack before!

"Dad!" yelled Crockett.

And then I knew. The baby in the video wasn't Jack.

It was me!

And I was acting like a vampire!

My throat got lumpy. "Did you know a man once ate six dozen doughnuts in six minutes and is the world record holder?"

Mom smiled. "Now do you understand, Katharine? *All* kids teethe and act like little monsters once in a while."

I slathered on my Luscious Lemon Lip Gloss and gave Jack a big kiss. "Sorry, Jack. Just because you act like a vampire doesn't mean you are one."

Then I confessed what had happened at the Halloween Costume Swap.

"I'm the only one without a costume," I said when I finished explaining.

"That's not true," said Crockett. "Vanessa didn't pick one either. She said she doesn't like Halloween."

"I thought every kid loved Halloween," said Aunt Chrissy.

Crockett shook his head. "Not Vanessa."

"I wonder why," said Dad.

Mom shrugged. "We'll probably never know."

But I knew!

And I knew exactly what to do about it!

❀ CHAPTER 8 ❀

Monsters-Be-Gone . . . For Good!

T he next morning, I walked into Mrs. Ammer's office and told her all about Jackula. "Now I know that vampires aren't real."

I thought Mrs. Ammer would laugh. But she didn't.

She ran her fingers through her pumpkin-colored hair. "When I was in first grade, I was convinced that the Boogeyman lived in my closet." She winked at me. "Thanks for being honest, Katharine. I was hoping you had a good reason to stuff those costumes into your bag."

She walked over to a coatrack and yanked the bag off.

"What are you going to do with all of them?" I asked. "There's oodles!"

"Mrs. Tracy and I are wearing two of them," she said. She dumped the costumes onto her desk. "Mrs. Curtin asked if she could borrow one. She lost her bunny costume, but she's going to wear her bunny slippers with it."

"We'll call her Bunnicula!" I laughed. "I love that book!"

"What about you?" said Mrs. Ammer. "Do you need one?"

I shook my head. "I'm making something for Vanessa and me."

Mrs. Ammer looked surprised. "Vanessa usually doesn't stay for the parade. It's nice of you to think of her."

She scooped the costumes up and shoved them back into the bag. Then she scribbled something on a pad of paper. "Have you told Vanessa that you no longer believe Jack's a pain in the neck?"

She chuckled at her own joke.

"Not yet, but I will, Mrs. Ammer." Then I decided to tell her one of Crockett's jokes. "Why don't mummies take vacations?"

"No clue," said Mrs. Ammer.

"They're afraid they'll relax and unwind!"

Then she told me a joke. "What kind of witch lives at the beach?"

Easy breezy! "A sand-witch!" I shouted.

I zip-a-zoomed back to class. I couldn't wait to tell Vanessa about Jack and our super-duper costumes. But I had to wait until lunchtime.

I sat next to Vanessa at the lunch table and said, "Here's your book back."

She grabbed it and shoved it underneath her tray. "What are you doing? Did anyone see it?"

"Nope," I said. Then I told her about the DVD and how all my proof went poof-a-roo. "Jack's just a normal baby. Like Frankie."

Vanessa didn't believe me.

"Monsters *are* real. Jack *is* Jackula. Look at his teeth!" Then, she bit into her apple and a wiggly tooth popped out! When she smiled, she had two pointy teeth! They looked like fangs!

Lily gasped. "You look like a vampire." She snatched Vanessa's thermos. "Is that *blood*?" She scooted down to the next seat and whispered, "Fang Face."

Sam looked over at Vanessa's teeth. "Weren't you born in Transylvania?"

"I'm *not* a vampire," whined Vanessa. She unscrewed the lid on her thermos. "I have cherry juice. My teeth are pointy." She banged her fist on the table. "Haven't you ever heard of *Pennsylvania*?" She twirled her hair. "Everyone is being silly."

"Everyone?" I asked.

She bit her lip. "Okay. I believe you. There's no such thing as monsters." She swallowed hard. "Right?"

"Right!" I shouted.

Then I told her about the costumes I was making. "Do you want to help? You're a fab-u-lo-so artist."

She gulped. "I haven't marched in the parade since kindergarten."

"It's fun," I said. "Except when the little monsters chase you."

Vanessa took a deep breath. "Monsters?"

"The kindergartners," I said. "They run around roaring and making all sorts of noise. But we don't have to worry. We'll be dressed up like Monsters-Be-Gone spray. We'll just zap, zap, zap them away!

❀ ❀ ❀

During the parade, lots of kids tried to scare us, but we sprayed them away. Every last one! My plan was per-fect-o!

When the parade was almost over, I spied Mom, Aunt Chrissy, and Jack standing next to Mrs. Garfinkle and Frankie.

Vanessa and I rush-a-rooed over. Jack and Frankie were dressed up as pumpkins. Frankie held a sign that said, Halloween is a real treat.

"Looks like you won't be needing your Monsters-Be-Gone spray for these pumpkins," said Mrs. Garfinkle.

Just then, I felt a tap, tap, tap on my shoulder. I turned around and saw our music teacher, Mrs. O'Neil.

"Hi, girls! I want you to meet my son. I named him after my favorite composer."

I looked at the baby. Then I turned toward Vanessa. "He sure is hairy."

The baby let out a noise so loud, we covered our ears.

"He howls like that a lot," said Mrs. O'Neil. "Sorry."

Vanessa and I stepped back. "What's his name?" I asked.

"Wolfgang Amadeus Mozart O'Neil," said Mrs. O'Neil. "But we call him Wolfie."

I put my hand on my forehead and joked, "We're doomed! Doomed!"

Vanessa laughed and looked up at the sky. "I wonder . . . is there a full moon tonight?"

We zoomed back in line and finished marching. We both knew there was nothing to worry about. After all, monsters aren't real . . .

Are they?